PUFFIN BOOK[illegible]
Editor: Kaye We[illegible]

LITTLE PETE STORIES

Little Pete, who first became popular on the B.B.C.'s *Listen with Mother* programme, is a tough self-reliant little four year old. He is always alone, except for his shadow, whom he treats as a friend, but he manages to make exciting adventures out of all his ordinary everyday encounters.

Through his eyes children will learn to look with pleasure and curiosity at their surroundings and also discover a good deal about the proper way to deal with the puzzling behaviour of grown-ups.

A really charming and rewarding collection for reading aloud to children of three, four and even five.

LEILA BERG

LITTLE PETE STORIES

Illustrated by
PEGGY FORTNUM

PENGUIN BOOKS

Penguin Books Ltd, Harmondsworth, Middlesex, England
Penguin Books Australia Ltd, Ringwood, Victoria, Australia

—

First published by Methuen 1952
Published in Puffin Books 1959
Reprinted 1963, 1965, 1966, 1968, 1969, 1970, 1971 (twice)

—

—

Made and printed in Great Britain
by Cox & Wyman Ltd,
London, Reading and Fakenham
Set in Monotype Baskerville

Contents

1

PETE AND THE CAR

ONCE upon a time, a little boy was walking down the road. His name was Pete.

It was a bright, sunny day, and Pete's shadow, very black was walking next to Pete on the pavement. Pete wanted very much to stand on his shadow's head, but he couldn't manage it. He tried a lot of times, jumping very quickly when he thought his shadow might not notice. But he couldn't do it.

He tried six times. Then he gave up. And his shadow went on walking quietly and blackly, next to him.

Now at that very moment, Pete saw a car. Of course, he had already seen dozens of cars. Black and green and red and cream, they had been whizzing down the road all the time he had been walking along.

But this car was standing quite still by the pavement. It was a yellow car, and the hood was down. There was no one in it.

Pete poked his finger in the radiator. Not right in, of course. That might spoil the car. Just in and out, to see how far it would go.

Then he took a stick and drew P (for Pete) in the dust on the car. Then he drew M (for

Motor Car) and S (for Stick). He wanted to do something (for Radiator), but he couldn't think what it could be.

After that, he peeped right into the open car. And his shadow climbed in front of him and sat right down on the seat. 'Well!' said Pete. 'What cheek,' said Pete.

Then Pete climbed over the door and he got in too. His shadow had politely moved up a bit, so Pete sat down next to it.

'Oo,' he said, 'what a bouncy car.' He bounced up and down two or three times. Then he pressed the hooter so as not to waste time. Peep. Peep-peep, Peep-peep. PEEEEP-peep. 'Out of the way!' shouted Pete, holding the steering-wheel. 'Out of the way! I'll run you all over! Mind out, you sillies! Get out of the way, can't you!'

The car was still standing by the pavement, but Pete was having a very exciting time. He pressed the hooter as hard as he could. It went on and on – PEEEE – and on and on – EEEE – and just before it had got to EEP, a man opened the front door and came down the steps, three at a time.

He looked very cross. 'Stop that,' he said. 'Get out of this car.'

Pete got out quickly. His shadow got out too.

'What's this?' said the man, pointing to the letters Pete had made on the car.

'That's P for Pete and that's M for Motor Car, and S for Stick – what I made them with. And I was going to do something (for Radiator – what I pushed my finger into) but I didn't know what it was.'

'It's R for Radiator,' said the man, still very cross.

So Pete picked up the stick and wrote R for Radiator on the car.

Then the man did something that made Pete really angry. He snatched Pete's stick out of his hand and threw it right away, as far as he could.

Pete was very cross indeed. 'You shouldn't do that,' he shouted. 'That was my stick, and you're not fair.'

But the man said: 'If you help me to wash the car down and make it shine, then you can get in the car, and I'll take you for a ride to a shop. And in the shop I'll buy you a notebook and a pencil, and you can write P for Pete as much as you like.'

'And M for Motor Car, and S for Stick, and R for Radiator?' said Pete.

'Yes. And W for Wash,' said the man. 'And D for Don't-shout-so-much.'

And he went into his garage, and brought out two big buckets of water and cloths. And Pete and the man sloshed the water over the car.

They sloshed it and swished it, and splashed it and swooshed it, and the water dripped all round the car and all over the road and the pavement and Pete's shoes. It was the most beautiful mess Pete had ever seen. And the car was polished clean and bright.

The man was very pleased. He put the buckets and the cloths away. And Pete ran very quickly to ask his Mummy if he could go in the man's car, because the man had told him to ask. When his Mummy saw who the man was, she said yes.

'You can get in now,' he said. So Pete got in, in the driver's seat.

'No, not there,' said the man.

'But I want to drive,' said Pete.

'Not now,' said the man. 'Another day.'

So Pete moved up, and his shadow moved up. The man sat down behind the steering-wheel. And the man's shadow sat on Pete's lap and Pete's shadow had to lean against the side of the car.

Peep! They were off. And that was how Pete got a new notebook and pencil, and learnt how to polish a car till it was shiny and yellow as a lemon junket. That was a good day.

THE BRIDGE

HERE is the bridge
Where I love to stop.
The cars go under,
The trains on top.

I stand on the pavement,
And watch them go,
The trains on top
And the cars below.

2

PETE AND THE STICK

ONE day, Pete was walking down the road with no one but his shadow, when he found a stick. It wasn't an ordinary kind of stick that anyone might find. It was almost a tree. It had branches growing from it, with green leaves on them, and it was very, very big.

Pete bent down to pick it up. His shadow bent down too.

'Silly,' thought Pete, noticing his shadow. 'There's no stick for you.' But Pete was wrong. There *was* a stick for his shadow, and the shadow picked it up when Pete picked up *his* stick. Now they each had one.

Pete's stick was very grand. It was so wide that it stretched right across the pavement from one side to the other. And when Pete marched along, holding it up in the air, no one could get by. Even his shadow had to walk behind.

Everyone else had to walk on the road, which made them rather cross. But Pete didn't notice.

Pete held his stick high up in the air, with the branches stretching out. And his shadow did the same.

Pete raced down the road. He was an aeroplane. Weeeeee! Everyone got very quickly out of the way.

Now he was an aeroplane curling about. WOOO-EEE-WOOOOO-EEE-OOO! No one would walk on Pete's side of the road now. Everyone crossed to the other pavement. Only his shadow stayed with him, for his shadow was being an aeroplane too.

‘Woooo,’ said Pete. ‘Woooeeeooo!’ And his shadow said nothing.

But after a while Pete was tired of being an aeroplanc. He thought he would hide his stick in the hedge, in a special place of his own. Then the next time he came down the hill, he would take it out, and be an acroplane again. So he looked for a special place.

He didn’t want a place where the stick would show too much, because he was quite sure that if anyone saw that stick in a hedge, they would pull it out at once, and be an aeroplane with it. So he found a place where the stick could pretend it was a tree, and look as if it were growing. 'Now wait!' said Pete very sternly. 'I'll be back soon.'

Just then the sun went behind a cloud and Pete's shadow disappeared. Pete's shadow was a fusspot and would never stay outside when the weather was dull. But Pete didn't mind. He was pretty certain the sun would come back again.

He went right up the hill by himself, and ran all the way down. Then he looked for his stick again.

It was still there, pretending to be a tree. Lots of real trees were there too. And Pete couldn't tell at all which was which.

The only way he could tell was by trying to pull each tree out. If it wouldn't come out, no matter how hard he pulled, then it was a real tree.

When he had pulled eleven real trees, a man came out of the garden. He was cross. 'What are you doing to my hedge?' he said very loudly.

'You shouldn't shout,' said Pete. 'I'm looking for my stick. It's pretending to be a tree.' And he started pulling more real trees.

'I don't see why you have to have this stick,' said the man crossly. 'Just manage without it.'

'I can't,' said Pete. 'It's for being an aeroplane.'

'Well, don't *be* an aeroplane,' said the man. 'Be a train.'

'I was a train this morning,' said Pete sadly.

'Well, be a car.'

'I can't be a car today.'

'Why not?' said the man.

'No petrol.'

'Well just be a good boy, and go away for heaven's sake.'

'I can't go away and leave my stick, can I? It's my stick and it belongs to me, and if I leave it it'll get spoilt and someone'll take it, and it'll get rained on. Even a cat might eat it up and then what d'you think?'

'Oh, all right,' said the man. 'I'll find it for you.' And he pulled and pulled. And Pete pulled and pulled. Till as last something came quite easily out of the bushes in the man's hands. 'That's my stick!' shouted Pete, and he grabbed it. 'WOOEEEOOO!'

'You might say thank you,' said the man.

'Thank you,' said Pete.

But just as Pete was starting to be an aeroplane again, someone pulled his beautiful stick out of his hand. He turned round quickly, and there was a dog.

'What cheek!' shouted Pete. 'Give me my stick!'

But the dog ran down the road, pulling the stick behind it. 'Leave it alone,' shouted Pete. 'You're making it dirty!'

'You shouldn't shout,' said the man.

'It's that dog. He's making me shout,' said Pete tearfully. 'He's a horrid dog and I hate him.'

The dog was sitting down on the pavement, with the stick by his side. His tongue was hanging out – huh huh huh – and he was looking at Pete.

'Now I'll get it,' said Pete, making horrible faces. And he dashed down the road. But the dog barked – oh oh oh – and picked up the stick and dashed away again.

'Horrid horrid dog,' said Pete, walking backwards towards the hedge again. Then he sat down on the wall and stuck his thumb in his mouth, because he felt very miserable.

'You shouldn't suck your thumb,' said the man.

'You shouldn't stand there letting that dog get my stick,' said Pete bitterly. 'You should help me. You know that, don't you?'

'Well, it's like this,' said the man. 'If I run after the dog, he'll run away. He thinks it's a game, you see.'

'That's a silly think,' said Pete. 'He must be a very silly dog to think such a very silly think!'

But the man said: 'You mustn't interrupt, or I'll forget what I'm saying. . . . There now, I've forgotten already. You see what you've done. You see.'

'You said he thinks it's a game,' said Pete.

'That's right,' said the man. 'He thinks it's a game if we chase him. But if, instead, you just bent down and picked up a stick – any stick will do,' he said quickly, 'just an ordinary straight stick with no leaves or branches at all – and threw it for the dog, he'd think that that was a better game, and he'd come and get the ordinary stick instead.'

'Would he really?' said Pete excitedly. 'Promise?'

'Well I can't exactly promise,' said the man. 'Only the dog can promise.'

'Dogs can't promise,' said Pete disgustedly. 'You are silly.'

'Well, anyway' – the man was getting cross again – 'anyway, I *think* that's what he'll do. You just try.'

So Pete picked up a very ordinary stick that was lying on the pavement, and he shouted: 'Here's a stick for you,' and he threw it as far as he could. Whoosh!

The dog dropped Pete's special stick and ran to get the new one. And quick as he could. Pete raced down the road to get his own stick back.

'There you are,' said the man, very pleased. 'What did I tell you!'

'That was a very good plan I made,' said Pete. 'Didn't I run *fast*!'

Then the man went inside because Pete's big stick with its wide branches was knocking him off the pavement.

And down the road again went Pete with his huge stick. And right at his side went the dog with his little stick; this was the kind of game he liked best of all.

Racing like two of the fastest aeroplanes in the world, they went whizzing together down the road. 'Wheeeeee!' shouted Pete. And just as they reached the bottom, the sun came out, and Pete's shadow popped up with its own stick. Now there were three of them.

That was a good day too.

3

PETE AND THE ROAD-ROLLER

ONE day, Pete was coming down the stairs backwards. He liked it better coming down that way. It was rather slow as there were a great many stairs, but Pete didn't mind. He held carefully on to the rails, and took his time.

He was nearly at the bottom when he heard a loud noise in the street. Glunk. Glunk. Glunk. Glunk.

'A road-roller!' shouted Pete. And he

turned quickly frontwards and rushed down the rest of the steps as fast as he could.

Down the street he dashed, just ahead of a new green road-roller. And his shadow dashed beside him.

His shadow knew nothing about staying on the pavement. It stretched out on the road, very long and black.

Pete stopped, so that the road-roller would run over his shadow. What will happen to it then? he thought. That will teach it to stand in the road, the silly.

Glunk, glunk, went the road-roller. Glunk.

But it didn't go over the shadow because the shadow stood up and leaned on the road-roller till it had passed by, then it fell down quietly on the road again. 'Bother,' said Pete. 'I'll try again.'

So Pete ran down the street and got in front again, so that the road-roller could run over his shadow this time. But the same thing happened. And Pete was rather disappointed.

Then Pete took an empty matchbox out of his pocket and threw it in front of the road-roller. Now what will happen, he thought. He put his hands to his ears and screwed up his face tight. He was sure there was going to be a tremendous crash.

But there wasn't any sound at all, except glunk, glunk, glunk. And when Pete opened his eyes again, there was his matchbox flattened out quietly, and the road-roller glunking down the road as if nothing had happened at all.

Pete ran after it again, and this time he took out of his pocket a soft, warm piece of Plasticine, and rolled it very quickly into a ball. He threw it under the road-roller and closed his eyes tight. 'I will count ten,' he said. 'One, two, three, four, five, six, seven, eight, nine – TEN!'

When he opened his eyes again there was

nothing on the road. Nothing at all. And the road-roller was glunking away with a bit of Plasticine stuck to it, rolling round and round and round.

Pete was very angry at this. 'Give me back my Plasticine!' he shouted. 'Give it me back, it's mine!'

He ran after the road-roller as fast as he could, shouting at the driver, and making horrible faces. 'What cheek!' he shouted. 'Look what you've done!' he shouted. 'You should look where you are going, shouldn't you?'

The driver couldn't hear a word Pete was saying. He tried not to take any notice for a bit because he had a lot of work to do. But when he saw what fierce faces Pete was making, he thought it might be important. So he put on the brake and stopped.

'Hello,' he said, 'what's up?'

'Hello,' said Pete, feeling very out of breath. 'Look what you've done!'

The driver leaned out, so that he could see right down the road behind the road-roller. There was nothing there. Everything was just

the same as usual. 'What *have* I done?' he asked, scratching his head.

'You've taken my Plasticine away on your roller,' said Pete. 'It was jolly good Plasticine. It was my best piece. I was going to make an elephant with it.'

'Was there a lot of it?' asked the driver.

'Of course there was,' said Pete. 'It was an enormous piece. Bigger than that house. Bigger than me even.'

'As big as my road-roller?'

'Bigger,' said Pete, sternly.

'Well,' said the driver. 'Where is it then?'

'It's underneath, of course,' said Pete. 'Underneath the roller, can't you see?'

'No, I can't,' said the driver.

'Of course you can't see if it's underneath,' said Pete. 'Silly!'

Pete and the driver looked at each other.

'I'll have to start her going again,' said the driver. 'Then we can get it.' He sat down in his seat and started the roller. Glunk, glunk, it turned again with a clatter.

'There it is,' shouted Pete. 'Stop! Stop!'

The driver jammed on the brake. But when

the roller stopped, the Plasticine had gone underneath again.

'Didn't you hear me say "Stop"?' said Pete severely.

'Of course I did,' said the driver. 'I stopped as soon as you said it.'

'No you didn't,' said Pete. 'You went on and on and on and on. And *now* look what's happened.'

'I'll start her again,' said the man. 'No need to get so excited.' Glunk went the roller.

'Stop! Stop!' shouted Pete. The roller stopped. But it was no good. The Plasticine was underneath again.

'Oh,' said Pete disgustedly. 'Bother it. Let *me* do it.' And he started to climb up the road-roller to get into the driver's seat.

'Here,' shouted the driver. 'You can't do that!' And he pulled Pete back by his legs.

Pete was very angry. 'You've broken my legs, and stretched my trousers, and bent my feet,' he shouted.

'Well,' said the driver. 'The Borough Council will be after you if you drive a roller, you know. It's not allowed.'

'Well *you* do it, don't you?' said Pete.

'I'm allowed to,' said the driver. 'I've got a special card saying I can.'

'Well, anyway,' said Pete, 'you should say you're sorry for breaking my legs.'

'Sorry,' said the driver.

Then the driver said, 'I'll try her again. Just once more. And this time you hold up your hand, like this, immediately the roller starts turning. See?'

'Like a policeman?' said Pete. 'All flat and stiff?'

'All flat and stiff,' agreed the driver. 'Ready now.'

And he started the roller again. Pete held up his hand immediately the roller moved. 'There it is,' cried Pete.

They both looked at the Plasticine. It was flattened out like a little white button on the roller. 'It's a very tiny piece for an elephant,' said the driver.

'I meant a baby elephant,' explained Pete. 'Anyway, I expect some has gone inside the roller.'

Then the driver climbed back into his cabin

quickly, because he was rather afraid Pete might want him to take the road-roller to pieces to see if there was any Plasticine inside. He set the roller going again. Glunk, glunk, glunk. And Pete ran in front.

Then do you know what Pete did? He rolled his Plasticine into a ball and threw it right in front of the roller again. And when it stuck, he ran beside it and watched it go round and round like a little white button, all over again.

That was another good day.

THE TRAM

WHEN I was younger
Than I am,
I went to Trowton
On a tram.

We made such a clanging
Banging din,
Just like a dustman
Emptying a bin.

And oh it was such a
Lovely feeling,
Sitting on top
Without a ceiling.

I wish I could sit
Up there again,
Next to the sun
And next to the rain.

But now there are no more
Trams to see. . . .
I'll tell my babies,
There used to be.

4

PETE AND THE RAIN

ONE day, it was pouring with rain. It poured and poured. Pete put on his raincoat with the hood, and his big Wellingtons, and went outside to see what was happening.

The rain was swishing down. It bounced on the pavement. It dripped from the gate. And it made huge puddles in bumpy places.

There was no one about but Pete. Everyone who could manage it was warm and dry indoors. Even Pete's shadow hadn't come out. It never came out in the rain.

But Pete didn't mind at all being alone. For over the road, in a huge puddle, boats were sailing. Pete was sure that they were boats.

The puddle was under a gate and hundreds of boats were sailing busily backwards and forwards. Pete stood and stared. He had never

seen such a thing before. He looked carefully both ways, then he crossed the road.

He splashed and plomped and plomped and splashed, to the other side. His Wellington boots squashed out the water from under his feet, and it splashed all round him. Now he could see they weren't boats at all. They were enormous bubbles.

The rain was dropping from the gate and as each drop fell into the puddle it turned into a bubble and sailed merrily along. It *was* exciting.

Pete crouched down beside the gate and watched. He tried to count the bubbles but they wouldn't stay still, and besides, new ones kept coming all the time. So he gave it up. Sometimes they sailed one behind another, like ducks swimming across a lake, in a tidy line. Sometimes they went round in a ring.

After a while Pete stood up and very carefully he put his foot on a bubble. It vanished. He did it again. Then in a minute he was jumping up and down in the puddle, splashing about in his boots, stamping on every bubble thc second it popped up in the water.

Then at last he waded out. And his Wellingtons were black and shiny with the wash they had had.

Now Pete saw that a river was running down the road. All along the gutter the rain had been carrying dead leaves along – leaves and sticks and papers as well. And some of the rubbish had stuck in the bars of the drains.

Now the drains were blocked up. And the rain went swirling gaily over them, not stopping at all to dip down between the bars as it ought to have done. Over the drains went the rain-water, racing along like a wide, deep river tumbling downhill.

Pete thought he saw a fish in the water. A very tiny fish. It popped up and down, and dodged between the leaves.

It was a black fish, thought Pete. But it wasn't, it was a little stick.

When Pete saw that it was only a stick, he didn't mind a bit. He ran along beside it and when it got stuck as it did sometimes, he helped it along with his finger. It sailed beautifully. Pete was very pleased with it.

Pete and the stick went right down the hill together. It was a long way.

Suddenly, near the bottom of the hill, Pete saw an old man poking about with a walking-stick. He poked in the drain and pushed all the rubbish off, and just as Pete's stick came sailing along, all the water started to go down the drain. Down went the stick. Flick! It was gone.

Pete was very upset. He was so upset he couldn't say a word. He just stared at the drain.

Then at last he said: 'Why did you do that? Now I've lost my sailing stick!'

'Your sailing stick?' said the old man.

'It sailed all the way down that hill,' said Pete.

'It *is* a very long way,' said the old man.

'It sailed for miles,' said Pete. 'For miles and miles. And now I've lost it.'

'I'm very sorry,' said the old man.

'Well, you shouldn't have done it,' cried Pete finding his voice. 'You were horrid.'

'I was clearing the drains,' explained the old man. 'If the rain keeps pouring down and the drains are stopped up, why there'd be water all over the place. We wouldn't be able to go anywhere at all.'

'We could use boats,' said Pete angrily.

'Who's got boats?' said the old man. 'I haven't. Have you?'

'We could make them,' said Pete scornfully.

'Course we could. My Daddy could make them.'

'Not for everybody, he couldn't,' said the old man. 'Everybody'd need a boat of their own. Dad would need a boat for going to work. Mum would need a boat for going shopping. You'd need a boat for going to play. Others'd need a boat for going to school. He couldn't make all those boats, you know. Couldn't possibly.'

'I don't care,' said Pete. 'You were very horrid to lose my sailing stick. What can I do now? I haven't got a sailing stick! I haven't got anything! And look at the rain! It's pouring and pouring – and it's all your fault.'

'I'll tell you what,' said the old man. 'I've got an idea.'

Pete said nothing. He just waited.

'You see that very special walking-stick,' said the old man. 'I can use it for all kinds of things, you know. And this morning I'm using it for clearing the drains. I *might* let you help me.'

'Help you clear the drains?' shouted Pete. 'Poking the stick between the bars? And pushing the leaves away? And letting the water go down?'

'Yes,' said the old man. 'I *might*. I'm not quite sure yet.'

'Oh *please*, *please*,' cried Pete, jumping up and down. '*Do* let me.'

'All right,' said the old man. 'I will. But you must stop splashing me. And you must stop shouting.'

'I will,' promised Pete. 'At least I'm not absolutely sure I'll remember but I'll try. Only I expect I'll forget.'

And he and the old man went right up the hill, poking the leaves off all the drains, and letting the water tumble in.

Right to the top they went, taking it in turns all the way, to make it quite fair. And when they had finished, the water slipped right down between the bars, the way it was meant to go.

And soon there was no river left at all. Just Pete, and the old man with a walking-stick.

That was another good day.

5

PETE AND THE TRICYCLE

One day, Pete went out on his tricycle to buy a lollipop.

All night long it had been raining and raining. But now the sun was shining, and the wind was blowing all over the pavements, blowing the rain away. The pavements were white and clean where the wind had dried them. And the big puddles, that were too deep for the wind to blow away, looked blue and white because the sky was shining in them.

Pete got on his tricycle and rode away. He felt important. He had never been shopping on his tricycle before.

'I'll ride through every puddle,' he said to himself. 'Then what d'you think!' And he nodded his head, to show he had quite made up his mind.

He rode right through the first puddle, and bits of it flew up in the air. But when he looked round the puddle was still there. 'But I *did* bounce it out,' said Pete, rather puzzled.

Behind his trike was a long black line. His wheel had made it, when it came out of the puddle. When Pete noticed it, he was pleased.

'I meant to do that,' he said. (But he hadn't really.)

So he rode right through the next puddle, with his black line shining behind him. And now when he looked round, instead of *one* black line there were three, because this

puddle was a very big one, and all three of the wheels had gone right into it.

'I'm an engine driver,' cried Pete. 'And those are my railway lines. Oooo! Ooooooo!'

And he rode his tricycle through every puddle he could see.

Sometimes it was a small puddle, and then there was only one railway line. And sometimes it was a middle-sized puddle, and then there were two railway lines. And sometimes it was a very big puddle, with plenty of sky in it, and then the whole tricycle went through it, and there were three railway lines.

Suddenly Pete remembered that he had

meant to go to the shop on the corner and buy a lollipop. He put his hand in his pocket to make sure his two pennies were still there. There was one of them – two of them. . . . Pete felt them each separately.

'It was good of me to remember,' he told himself. 'I'm a jolly good rememberer.' And he nodded his head thoughtfully, and rode off up the road, very straight and properly.

As he pedalled along, a tiny fat kitten came pouncing out of a doorway. The kitten ran sideways, up to Pete's tricycle, doing a funny

little dance, and Pete laughed at her. 'You funny little kitten,' he said. 'You funny one.'

But the kitten didn't understand about tricycles. She suddenly put out a paw and patted the tricycle wheel, and it hurt her foot. The kitten cried and ran away. And Pete put his brake on hard, and sat quite still, feeling very upset.

Just then a lady ran out of the house and cried: 'Oh, you've run over my kitten. I saw you from the window. Poor little kitty.'

'Well,' said Pete, 'I didn't do it on purpose.

She was trying to tickle my tricycle. She wanted to play.'

And Pete rubbed his face with the sleeve of his coat.

The lady looked at Pete. Then she said: 'I think I've made a mistake. You don't look like a boy who would run over kittens on purpose. I believe you're very fond of kittens. You look like a good driver too.'

Pete sniffed.

'Blow your nose,' said the lady. 'Would you like to see our three kittens? We have a white one, a black one, and one that is black and white mixed together.'

Pete blew his nose in a very big handkerchief, and wiped his face. Then he wiped his sleeve dry again.

'Oh, yes please, I would,' he said. 'Can I?'

So he left his trike in the hall, and went into the kitchen, where the three kittens were playing on the rug.

He took an old bus ticket out of his pocket and screwed it up in a twist, and all the kittens ran after it when he threw it.

They hopped and they pranced and they

jumped and they danced. And all the time they held their little tails up stiff and straight and quivery in the air.

Even the kitten who had hurt her paw, the black and white kitten, played just as gaily as the others. And that made Pete feel much better.

'I expect she's a bit of a fusspot,' explained Pete to the lady. 'Baby things generally are fusspots. I'm not a fusspot. I'm big.

'And I'll be very careful when I come past

this house next time, in case she comes out again. You don't have to worry. I'm a very good driver.'

Then he said good-bye, and went out of the house slowly, walking backwards so that he could see the kittens until the last moment. He had remembered about the lollipop.

'I'll come again,' he called to the kittens. 'I'm just going to a shop.'

'You can come after dinner,' said the lady. 'If your Mummy lets you.'

Pete was getting on his trike when a big man poked his head out of a window.

'See our kittens?' he said.

'Yes,' said Pete.

'Like 'em?' said the man.

'Yes,' said Pete again.

'Good,' said the man, and banged down the window again. Pete waited for a minute or two, but the man didn't come back again. So Pete rode away.

Then he remembered about the lollipop again. He rode on to the shop and bought a little green one. Then he rode slowly back, sucking it, while he and the trike got stickier and stickier. And Pete thought to himself about what had happened.

Then at last he said to himself, 'Anyway, I found three kittens.'

'And I can go another day.

'And I will.

'And I'll take them a marble to play with.'

Then he and his shadow waved their lollipops, feeling happy again now, and rode right through a puddle.

And this time, it was such an enormous puddle, with sky and clouds and even seagulls in it, that there was room for Pete and his shadow as well.

So it ended up quite a good day after all.

WASHING DAY

LUCKY old Anna,
Elbows in the froth,
Stirring up the soap-suds,
Squeezing out the cloth.
We'll help Anna,
Don't you run away,
We'll all take a hand in
Anna's washing-day.

Rub-a-dub the washing,
What a lot of dirt!
Here's my woolly stocking,
There's Rosetta's skirt.
Wring out the cottons,
Squeeze out the wool;
Pile it all together till
The tin bath's full.

Shake out the washing,
Hang it on the line.
The overalls are Billy's.
The pinafores are mine.

Blow, wind, blow it!
Make the washing fly!
Make it dance the hornpipe till
The whole lot's dry!

6

PETE AND THE FLOWERS

One day, Pete was walking along with only his shadow, when he saw a garden filled to bursting with flowers. They were every colour you could imagine, those flowers. Red and yellow and purple and orange and blue. And white too.

There were so many of them that some were peering right out over the low hedge, and seemed to be saying to Pete: 'Just look at me! Look!'

Pete stopped and stared. He liked flowers.

One of the flowers, a big nodding comfy-looking one, was looking right into Pete's face. Very carefully he put out one finger and touched it.

At that very second someone slammed up a

window in the house with a big crash, and someone shouted: 'Leave those flowers alone!'

Pete had a terrible fright. He snatched back his finger. Then he stood stock still, not moving at all. He thought he was going to cry.

But just then a side-door opened, and a man came down the path with a broom. He was surprised to see Pete with his face near the flowers. And when he came closer and saw Pete looked very upset, he stopped.

'What's the matter?' said the man.

Pete said nothing for a minute. Then he said, 'She shouted, "Leave those flowers alone!" She gave me a fright.'

'Do you mean you were *picking* our flowers?' said the man.

'I was touching it,' said Pete. 'I was touching it because it was so purple. I wasn't taking it.'

He stopped, and the man thought for a moment. Then the man said, 'I'm sorry she shouted. I expect she didn't know.'

Pete was feeling better. 'Well, she shouldn't shout,' he said. 'It's horrid to shout.'

'I know,' said the man. 'You're quite right.

I never shout. But there's one thing you ought to know – you shouldn't say "she" all the time. It isn't nice. You should say "the lady in the house".'

'I know,' said Pete. 'I never say "she".'

The man looked at the big purple flower that Pete liked so much. 'Do you know what that's called?' he said. 'It's a hollyhock.'

'A lollipop?' said Pete, laughing.

'No, a hollyhock!'

'You said a *lollipop*,' Pete insisted.

'I didn't say anything of the kind,' argued the man.

'Well, what's that flower over there, then?' said Pete. 'The pinky one?'

'That's a rambling rose.'

'An *angry nose*?' cried Pete.

'I didn't say that at all. I said a "rambling rose".'

'There! You said it again!' shouted Pete triumphantly.

The man sighed. 'Would you like to help me in the garden?' he said. 'We could sweep up the leaves, and collect the weeds, and make a huge pile. And then we could light a fire.'

'A real one?' said Pete. 'With fireworks?'

'No fireworks,' said the man. 'Just a fire.'

'Just three fireworks,' said Pete.

'No,' said the man.

'Two fireworks then,' said Pete. 'One for you and one for me.'

'No fireworks at all,' said the man.

'Well, only one firework, a teeny weeny one like this' – Pete put his finger and thumb together very tight to show how teeny.

'Look,' said the man, 'this isn't a Guy

Fawkes fire. This is a fire-for-burning-garden-rubbish. I don't generally have a fire at all this time of the year. I was doing it specially for you. If you hadn't come along I wouldn't be bothering about it at all. But, of course, if you're going to go on and on and on about fireworks, then we'd better not have a fire.'

'All right,' said Pete. 'We'll just have a fire. And we can have treacle toffee.'

'No!' said the man. And he was just going to say a whole lot more, but Pete said, not caring at all, 'You don't have to worry. I'm not going to make a fuss. What are you worrying about?'

So without saying another word, the man gave Pete his broom, and bent down to pick weeds.

'There's one!' cried Pete. He was just starting to pull it up – a bunchy, green, grassy-looking thing it was – when the man grabbed his hand. 'No,' cried the man. 'That's not a weed!'

'It's just the same as the one *you're* pulling up,' said Pete, rather upset.

'No it isn't. Look, the leaves are diffcrent.'

'Well, they're baby leaves. When they've grown up, they'll be exactly the same,' cried Pete. 'You won't let me do anything. You said I could do things and now you won't let me do anything. And you're shouting.'

'I'm not doing anything of the kind,' said the man.

'Yes you are,' said Pete. 'You shouted very loud when you said "No" just now, and you said you didn't ever shout, and you do, and you've given me a headache, and you won't let me do anything!'

'Will you let me speak?' said the man. 'Do you mind if I say something now?'

'No,' said Pete. 'But say it soft.'

‘All I was going to say,’ said the man, ‘is that I was hoping you would sweep the leaves with my special broom, while I get on with the weeding.’

Pete thought for a moment. He was just going to argue a little, when the man said quickly: ‘It makes a lovely noise. A sort of *swish, swish* noise.’

‘Does it?’ said Pete. And he tried it.

It was a big broom, and sometimes Pete

tried to sweep with the broom and sometimes the broom tried to sweep with Pete. But at last Pete found the right way to do it, and then he said: 'No, it doesn't.'

'Doesn't what?' said the man, with his face near the weeds.

'It doesn't go *swish, swish*,' said Pete. 'It goes *crush, crush-sh*.'

'So it does,' agreed the man.

'What are those big flowers called?' said Pete.

'Those are gladioli,' said the man.

'Rolypoly?' said Pete.

'I didn't say that,' said the man. 'I said *gladioli*.'

'There, you said it again!' said Pete, delighted.

And Pete and the man laughed together, and felt very good friends.

They made a big heap of weeds and leaves, and they found some paper too. The man lit it very carefully, and let Pete blow out the match.

Then Pete put his hands in his pockets, two pockets in his trousers, and one in his shirt, and he took out all the bus tickets he had been saving for days and days. There were forty-seven of them. And he threw them all on the blazing fire.

If one fell to the ground in front of the fire, he left it there, not wanting to go too close to the fire, because the man said the fire was for burning the weeds and the leaves, and not for burning Pete.

Pete's shadow loved the fire. It danced up and down in the flickering light. Sometimes it

crouched right down on the ground by Pete's feet, and sometimes it jumped right up like the tallest giant in the world.

How the fire smoked and crackled! And scarlet sparks rode up on the smoke half-way to the sky.

That was another good day.

7

PETE AND THE LETTER

One day, Pete was walking along, trying not to tread on the lines between the paving stones. He walked very carefully, sometimes taking tiny steps, sometimes making big strides. 'When I've trodden on twenty lines,' Pete said to himself, 'I'll turn into an elephant. An enormous elephant with floppety ears.'

So he walked along very carefully, watching the pavement. 'One,' he said, and, 'oh bother, *two*.' And his shadow stayed behind him so as not to get in the way.

It was a beautiful October morning, the day Pete was an elephant. Everything was golden. The trees were golden in the sun, and the roads were a pale, smooth, frosty gold.

There were heaps of fallen leaves on the pavement. Pete shuffled his feet through them. He carried the leaves in little piles on his shoes. 'How long can I keep them like that, I wonder?' he said to himself. But they always slipped off in the end, one by one, and left his shoes dusty and grey.

'I will drop some on my shadow when it isn't looking,' thought Pete. 'That will be a surprise for it. I wonder how it will get out again.' So he kicked some leaves over his shadow. But his shadow guessed what Pete was going to do. Very quickly it got out of the way, just in time, and it tramped right over the leaves. 'What cheek,' said Pete. 'Those are *my* leaves.'

There was a bright-yellow leaf lying on the

pavement, such a bright, thick yellow that it looked as if someone had covered it with poster paint from one of the little pots he had at home. Pete picked it up and stared at it. He had a feeling he would like to know how such a bright-yellow leaf *tasted.* And he was just putting it in his mouth when he remembered it was probably dirty, so he dropped it again. Scrunch, scrunch, went his feet through the dry leaves.

Now there were no leaves at all. The pavement had been swept clean. So Pete was striding over the lines again, playing his elephant game. The stones were all different shapes and sizes, and that made it very hard. Besides, Pete was counting the cracks as lines too, and there were plenty of them. 'Three-four – *bother*, five, six-seven-eight-nine-ten.' He was getting nearer and nearer and nearer to being an elephant. So his shadow kept carefully behind him.

Pete was watching the pavement lines so very carefully, he didn't look at all where he was going. A sort of car came out of a gate, like a chair on wheels, and Pete almost fell into it.

He overbalanced, and his feet trod all over the place before he managed to stand straight again. 'You've turned me into an elephant!' he cried.

'You don't look like an elephant,' said the lady who sat in the chair.

'You've turned me into an elephant!' Pete shouted. 'You made me tread on hundreds and *millions* of lines, and now I'm an elephant and I wasn't going to be an elephant till I got to the top of the hill, so I could run all the way down!'

'I'm very sorry. But you weren't looking

where you were going. And my leg is all bandaged up, and you might have hurt it.'

'Did I?' said Pete.

'No,' said the lady. 'Next time I come out of this gate, I'll sound my horn.'

'Have you really got a horn?' said Pete.

'Of course,' said the lady. 'Will you post a letter for me?'

'Show me the horn,' said Pete.

'But will you post a letter for me?'

'Is this it?' said Pete.

'But *please*, *will* you post my letter?'

'Can I honk it?' said Pete.

'If you post a letter for me,' said the lady, 'you can honk it when you come back.'

Now Pete was worried. 'But I'm being an elephant,' he said. 'I have to stay on the pavement and be careful about the lines. I can't go posting letters *now*.'

'But you meant to go up the hill anyway,' said the lady. 'The letter-box is only on the top of the hill. And that's where you said you wanted to change into an elephant and run all the way down.'

'But you've made me turn into an elephant

already,' said Pete sternly. 'You made me tread on millions of lines. A thousand – twenty – million.'

'Oh no I didn't,' cried the lady. 'You only trod on one.'

'Which one?' said Pete.

'That one,' said the lady, pointing. 'The one near the gate.'

Pete bent down and looked at it. And his shadow bent down too. Yes, it *looked* as if it had been trodden on.

'Did I really only tread on that one?' said Pete. 'Wasn't that clever of me?'

'So now,' said the lady, 'you'll post my letter, won't you? Just at the top of the hill.'

'All right,' said Pete. 'Was it seven I was up to?' And off he went, counting all the way.

The lady watched him. When he got to the top of the hill, he shouted: 'Twenty!' and began to charge down again as fast as he could. And his shadow raced in front, for fear of being trodden on.

'But you didn't post my letter,' said the lady, sadly.

'Didn't I?' said Pete. And he looked at the

letter, still in his hand. He thought a minute. Then he said: 'Elephants don't post letters,' and he gave it back to her.

'Oh, circus elephants do,' cried the lady quickly.

'Do they really?' said Pete, very interested.

'Oh yes,' cried the lady. 'I know they do. Very clever circus elephants.'

'Shall I be one?' said Pete. 'Shall I be a circus elephant? I'll go up the hill doing a very funny dance. I'll go round and round, and do funny things with my feet. And when I get to the top I'll post the letter.'

'I'll watch,' said the lady. 'And I'll clap.'

'All right,' said Pete. 'But you mustn't clap till I tell you to.'

Off went Pete, turning round and round, and giving a little hop on one foot now and then. Long before he reached the top, he was getting so dizzy, he was turning round more than he wanted to. He was tottering about all over the pavement, and the lady, who was watching him, felt quite worried. As for his shadow, it didn't know whether it was safest in front of Pete or behind him, it was so muddled.

But at last Pete reached the letter-box. He sat down on the pavement in front of it, and put the envelope in his mouth. But he couldn't reach the letter-box at all that way.

So he stood up, with the envelope still between his teeth, and waved his head slowly, this way and that. Then at the last minute, he took the letter out of his mouth, stood on his tiptoes, and popped it in the box. 'Clap!' he shouted.

The lady clapped as hard as she could.

Pete raced right down the hill back to her. 'Was it a good circus?' he said.

'Lovely. And I saw how fast you ran, too.'

'Did you? I can run faster than I did then. I can run as fast as – that!' And he swished his hand right through the air.

'Can you?' said the lady. 'I couldn't.'

'I expect you can when your leg's better,' said Pete. 'Next week, we'll have a race. You might even *beat* me. You *might*.' He nodded his head encouragingly.

Then off he went, doing his elephant dance all over again, because it was such a good one.

But when he had gone a little way off, the lady called him back. 'You can honk the horn, you know,' she said, 'because you posted my letter.'

'So I can,' said Pete, most surprised at himself. 'I forgot about that.' He gave it one little honk, a short one, just to see how the horn sounded. Then he gave it a very long one, to see how the *honk* sounded. It sounded very good both ways, but the long one was better.

And that was another good day.

8

PETE AND THE LADYBIRD

ONE day, Pete found a matchbox. It was an empty matchbox, so Pete started to look for something to put in it.

He looked very hard all over the pavement. When he saw his shadow standing beside him, he said to his shadow: 'You look too.' So his shadow looked too.

A lady saw Pete bent over, looking. She stopped and asked him: 'Have you lost something?'

Pete straightened up. He shook his head. 'No, thank you,' said Pete. And he went on looking.

The lady was not in a hurry so she stayed beside him. Pete looked all over the pavement. Then he started looking in the gutter. At last the lady said: 'Why are you looking, if you haven't lost anything?'

Pete turned his head. He said to her: 'I'm looking for something to put in my matchbox, because there's nothing in it.' And he went on looking, and took no notice of her at all, because he was very busy.

She was just going to go far away, because she could see how busy he was, when she saw a feather come floating down from the sky. She reached out her hand, and caught it.

'Look,' she said. And she gave it to Pete.

'It's part of an eagle,' he said. 'I mean a seagle.' And he nodded his head, and put the feather in his matchbox.

But the feather wouldn't fit. It was much too big.

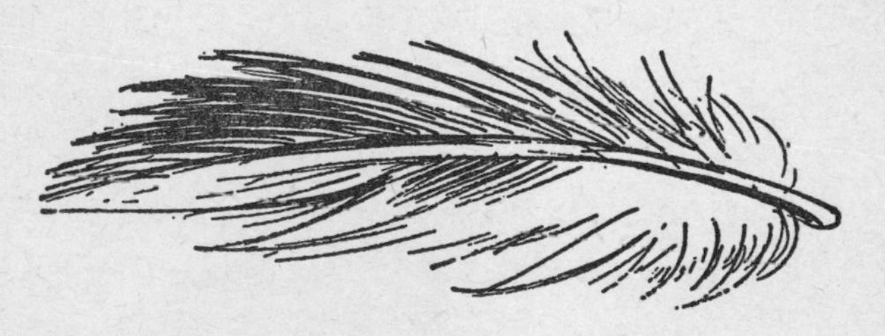

'Bother,' said Pete. 'We'd better give it back,' he said.

He stared up into the sky with its white racing clouds. There were three or four birds flying round and round. One of them was crying. 'I think it's that one,' said Pete. 'He's looking for it.' And he put the feather on his hand, and blew it. It sailed up, up into the air, and up into the sky. It was a very windy day. 'I hope the seagle caught it,' said Pete. 'It was his tail, I expect.' And he went on looking.

Now he found a holly leaf. It was a baby holly leaf, with soft baby prickles that didn't hurt at all. Pete liked it because it was so little, and green and shiny, and because its prickles were soft and tickly, and didn't hurt. He tried it in the matchbox, and it was just right.

'Good,' said Pete. 'It's the same long.'

'I think you mean the same length,' said the lady.

'I know,' said Pete. 'That's what I said.' And he shut the lid, and put the box in his pocket.

Then the lady went away, because there was

nothing else to help with. 'Good-bye,' she said, and Pete said good-bye, too.

The wind was blowing the clouds over the sun; one minute it was bright, one minute it was dull.

Pete began to play a game called Shadow-BANG. The way he played it was like this.

He stood on the pavement, with his legs wide apart. Then very suddenly, keeping his legs stiff, he bent down and looked between them and shouted 'Shadow-BANG'. And sometimes his shadow was there, and then Pete won. And sometimes his shadow wasn't, and then Pete didn't win *absolutely*, only almost.

Now just as Pete had his head between his legs, and was opening his mouth to shout 'Shadow-BANG' for the nineteenth time, a ladybird came along the pavement. She was behind Pete, and Pete saw her through his legs. She came nearer and nearer. And as she got nearer, Pete moved his head back through his legs again, till he was simply standing on the pavement with his hands on his knees, staring at a ladybird.

She was an orange-coloured ladybird with three big spots. 'Hello, ladybird,' Pete said, as she went past his shoe. But she didn't answer.

Pete very carefully kneeled down on the pavement, and put his finger in front of the ladybird. She thought about his finger. Pete could see her thinking. Then just as he thought she didn't like his finger, she decided that she did. She climbed on it, and Pete slowly stood up.

Then he walked along carefully. He was taking the ladybird home.

He was looking so hard at the ladybird as he

walked along carefully, that he bumped right into a window-cleaner. The window-cleaner was propping up a ladder against the wall.

'Look out!' he shouted. 'Where d'you think you're going?'

But Pete was staring at his finger. The ladybird had gone. She had opened her wings and flown straight into the wind. And now he couldn't see her anywhere.

He turned to the window-cleaner. He was very upset. 'You've lost my ladybird,' he said tearfully. 'I was taking her home and she was going to live in my matchbox, and now she's gone and she'll get lost, and its all your fault –

'Hush,' said the man, flapping his duster in front of Pete's face.

Pete was rather surprised at that, and he hushed.

'Were you telling me off about something?' said the window-cleaner.

'Yes, I am telling you off,' said Pete. 'I'm telling you off because you lost my ladybird and she'll get lost and I was taking her home –'

'Wait a minute,' said the window-cleaner. 'It's a funny thing you should be telling *me* off, because I was telling *you* off. What's the idea of bumping into me, and not even saying you were sorry? You might have sent this ladder right through the window, you know, and smashed all the glass and everything. If only you'll look where you're *going*,' he said, 'I'll look where you're *coming*.'

Pete laughed. Then the man said: 'Shall I tell you something?'

'What?' said Pete.

'I think your ladybird was glad to fly away. I don't mean she didn't like you,' he said quickly, because he could see Pete was going to get cross again. 'I expect she liked you very much, but really she wanted to fly about in the sun. She was just walking along with you because she liked you. And then it was time for her to go.'

'I know,' said Pete. 'It isn't time for me to go. Can I help you clean windows?'

'Well, just for a little bit,' said the window-cleaner.

So Pete stood on the second rung of the ladder, and cleaned a little piece of window, just as big as his head. And the window-cleaner did the rest because he was used to it.

And when they had finished, all the blue sky shone in the window and the sun came and sat in it.

'Didn't we make it shiny?' said Pete.

That was a good day, too.

THE FUNNY OLD TRAIN

CH Ch Ch goes the funny old train,
Under the bridge and back again.
Puffing, chuffing, as hard as it can,
Carrying coals for the driver-man.

Where do you take your coal so fine,
Clickety, clackety, down the line?
Where do you take your big load to?
But the funny old train just answers Ooooo!

9

PETE AND THE WHISTLE

ONE hot sunny day, when Pete's shadow looked much blacker than usual, and followed him around wherever he went, Pete found a crowd of men at the end of his street. They had nothing on but their work-trousers and plimsolls, and they were digging, digging, digging, in the hot sun.

'What are you doing?' asked Pete.

‘We’re building a house,’ said one of them.

Pete was quiet for a minute. Then he said: ‘Tell me what you’re *really* doing.’

‘We’re building a house,’ said the man again. ‘Honestly we are.’

Now Pete was very angry.

‘But houses go up, not down,’ he cried. ‘You can’t *dig* a house. You can dig potatoes, or worms, or something that you hid there last time, but how can you dig a house! *What* are you doing? Tell me!’

‘Well,’ said the man, ‘if you’ll listen very carefully – and very quietly – and leave my spade alone – I’ll explain to you.’ And he wiped his hands on his trousers, for they were feeling rather sore and sticky.

And because Pete could see that what the man was going to tell him would be the truth, he stopped being angry and listened.

‘Now, this hole here,’ said the man, ‘this hole that we’re digging, is for standing the house in. When we build the wall of the house, we start it inside the hole, so that it stands up strong and steady.

‘Why, if we built the wall right on top of

the ground, without digging this hole first, as soon as the wind came along it'd blow the whole lot flat. One puff, and there'd be no house left.'

'Like the three little pigs?' said Pete. 'Like "*I'll huff and I'll puff*"?'

'That's right,' said the man. '"*I'll huff and I'll puff and I'll blow your house down.*" That's why we have to dig a hole for the walls to stand in.'

And he took up his spade again, and went on digging. And Pete went on watching.

When Pete thought he had seen enough of how the digging looked from one side, he thought he would see how it looked from the other side. So he jumped across the hole, because it was still only a little one. And his shadow jumped too.

But Pete's shadow was a silly. It fell in the hole.

'Dig my shadow!' shouted Pete. So the man took up a spadeful of Pete's shadow, and tried to lift it up and put it near Pete. But the shadow fell off the spade and lay in the hole again. 'Bother,' said Pete. And the man said

nothing because he was very hot; he just went on working.

Pete wanted to help. He said to the man: 'I'm a jolly good digger. I dig jolly fast. Shall I help?'

But the man said 'No!'

'No *thank you*, you mean,' said Pete sadly.

'No thank you,' said the man, and went on digging.

Suddenly, just behind him, a terrible noise started. It was like the noise a giant motor bike would make. It made all the ground shake.

Pete turned round quickly. He saw a man working a machine which made a hole in the ground. The man had a loose pullover on and it shivered when the man's arms shivered with the machine.

'Can I do that?' said Pete, but the man could not hear him.

'Can I do it?' cried Pete, but the machine shouted louder than Pete – and the man did not hear a word.

Now another man came by, pushing a wheelbarrow. He filled it full of bricks, then he pushed it away.

When he came again, Pete said: ‘I can do that. I can put the bricks in. I’m jolly strong.’

‘All right,’ said the man. ‘You can help. But you must be very careful not to drop one on your toe.’

‘Course I won’t,’ said Pete scornfully. ‘Shall I show you how I won’t? I’ll walk like this.’ And he put his heels together and turned his toes right out, so that a brick would fall in the space between, and he walked like Charlie Chaplin. ‘Now I can’t drop a brick on my toe, can I?' he said. And the man said, no, he couldn't.

So the three of them filled up the barrow, the man, and Pete, and Pete's shadow. At least, Pete's shadow *seemed* to be helping, even though he didn't make the barrow any fuller. And when the bricks were tidily piled together, and there was no room for any more, the man said to Pete, 'You can ride on top.'

'Really and truly?' said Pete.

'Really and truly, and absolooly,' said the man.

'You mean absolutely,' said Pete, laughing.

'So I do,' said the man.

Then Pete sat on top of the bricks and the man pushed it.

It was the first time Pete had ridden on a barrow full of bricks. It was a bit knobbly, but not very, because the bricks were piled very tidily.

As for Pete's shadow, there was no room for it on the barrow. So it sat on the ground, and pretended it was having a ride in a different barrow, with black bricks in it.

When Pete got off the wheelbarrow, an

enormous machine had started working. It was shovelling up sand in one place, and piling it up in another. It was very big and very clever and very quick.

Pete watched it for a while, and thought. Then he put his hand in his pocket and took out a whistle. He threw it on the ground and waited. The machine won't want my whistle, he thought. I wonder what it will do.

But the machine didn't care. Quick as a wink, it picked up the whistle. Then it emptied it on the pile of sand.

'Don't do that!' shouted Pete angrily to the machine. And he ran as fast as he could to get his whistle back. But a man grabbed him by his overalls, and held him tight.

The man was very cross.

'That's a very silly thing to do,' he shouted. 'You might get a whole load of sand on top of you. Go away at once.'

'Let go of me!' cried Pete. 'I want my whistle! You're pinching me! That machine's taken my whistle and I want it back. Look at it, look!'

The man looked. And just as he looked, the

machine dropped another load of sand right on top of Pete's whistle.

'There now,' said Pete bitterly. 'Look what it's done. Beastly old machine! And it's your fault for stopping me getting it.' And he put his thumb in his mouth, because he was very unhappy.

'Well,' said the man, holding Pete very firmly, 'we can't get it now. It'll be made into cement soon, and used to build the house.'

'My whistle will?'

'That's right,' said the man. 'And when this house is built, and people are living in it, with curtains up at all the windows and smoke coming out of the chimney, then you can say to everyone. "That house is sitting on my whistle"!'

'Yes,' said Pete, brightening up. 'That's what I'll say. I'll say, "Get off my whistle, house, or I'll push you over"!'

He thought for a minute, then he said: 'Will my whistle always be underneath the house? For ever and ever?'

'For ever and ever,' said the man.

'Then it'll get spoilt,' said Pete. 'It won't

be nearly so good when the house has been sitting on it.'

'No,' agreed the man, 'it won't be so good for *whistling*. But it'll be very good for telling people about.'

'Yes,' said Pete, 'it will be good for telling.' He thought for a bit. Then he said: 'I'll start telling people now.'

And he tramped away over the bumpy ground, by the heaps of bricks, and the sand, and the wheelbarrows, and all the men in their dusty working trousers. And his shadow walked behind and fell in all the holes because it never looked where it was going.

'Silly old shadow,' said Pete.

Then he said: 'I'm glad *I'm* not made into cement. I'm glad the house won't be sitting on *me*. *Jolly* glad!' And he nodded his head to himself.

And away he ran.

That was another good day!

PETE AND THE SPARROW

ONE day, Pete was walking up the hill. It was a lovely bright spring morning, and the birds were singing as loudly as they could.

His shadow walked very blackly on the wall beside him, but Pete took no notice of it today.

For it was springtime, and new exciting things were happening every day.

Suddenly Pete noticed a cat creeping slowly and quietly up a tree. He stopped to watch it. He liked climbing trees, too.

But when Pete watched he could see the cat wasn't playing. It was going somewhere special. It was a busy cat.

'What are you doing up there?' he called. But the cat only went on climbing.

And now Pete saw it was trying to catch

some birds who were talking together on the farthest branch.

'Come down at once, you naughty cat!' he called. 'Leave them alone.'

But the cat took no notice at all. It crept carefully along the branch.

'I'll be cross with you!' shouted Pete.

But just at that moment, the birds flew up in the air, all together. They did it so suddenly, and their wings made such a loud noise, that the cat nearly fell off the branch.

'There!' said Pete.

'You see!' said Pete.

'What did I tell you!' said Pete. And he went on his way.

He was glad the birds had flown away from the cat, and as he went he sang to himself a happy song that he had made up.

'Spring ter-ring, ter-ring,
Spring ter-ring, ter-ring,
Ter-ring,
Ter-ring,
Buttercups and daisies.'

Now he walked along a low wall, balancing himself carefully. He was a slow goods train, chuffing along, taking tractors to a farm.

All at once, he saw there was a bird on the wall in front of him.

'Oooooo!' went Pete the goods train. 'Peep-peep.'

But the bird didn't move. And Pete, who had expected the bird to fly away, almost lost his balance, trying to stop in time.

That gave him a fright. 'You silly old bird!' he shouted. And he jumped in the air, just a little jump on top of the wall, to shoo the bird away. But it still didn't move.

Pete looked at it. It was a very little bird.

He sat down on the wall, and put his face

quite close to it. The bird blinked its bright eyes at him.

Very slowly Pete put out a finger and stroked the little bird on the head. It was soft and warm and nobbly.

Then he put out his finger and did it again, because he had never done such a thing before. Then for a long time he looked right into the bird's eyes, and the bird looked at him.

Then he jumped off the wall, and started to walk up the hill again.

But just in front of him, a man was standing, staring into a tree, staring and staring. So Pete stopped.

'What are you looking at?' said Pete politely.

The man didn't answer.

Pete looked hard at the tree, but there didn't seem to be anything special to see. 'What are you looking at?' said Pete again.

But the man still said nothing.

Now Pete was cross. 'It's very rude not to tell people what you're looking at, when you're looking at a tree,' he said, 'when they're very polite and keep asking and asking, and keep on waiting for you to tell them.'

The man turned round. 'I'm looking at a bird,' he said.

'I was looking at a bird before,' said Pete. 'I put my face quite close to it, and I stroked its head. Is yours an eagle bird?'

But the man said nothing. He just looked into the tree. 'Mine was an eagle bird,' said Pete.

Then the man said: 'Did you honestly and truly *stroke* a bird?'

'Yes,' said Pete. 'I told you. I stroked its

head with my finger. It sat on the wall, and it nearly made me fall off. What cheek,' he said, 'sitting on the wall like that, making people nearly fall off. I might have had to have a plaster, you know!'

'Show me the bird,' said the man.

But Pete said to him quietly, 'You know what you should say, don't you?'

'What should I say?' asked the man.

'You should say, "Please", shouldn't you?'

'Please show me the bird,' said the man.

So Pete took his hand, and they went to the wall and found the bird. It was still sitting there. The man picked it up in his hand, and held it gently in his fist, with its face sticking out at the top. And Pete stroked it again, wondering how it could be so soft *and* so nobbly at the same time. Then he put his cheek against its face in case it wanted to whisper something. But it said nothing.

'It's a baby bird,' said the man. 'That's the mummy bird who's making all that fuss in the tree. She's calling him.'

'Why doesn't he go then?' said Pete. 'Can't he hear her?'

And the man said: 'Why, he can't fly properly yet. He flew *down* from his tree, because he was trying very hard. And besides it's easier to come down. But going up is difficult.' And he walked back to the tree, with the tiny bird in his fist. And Pete ran in front.

'Here he is,' cried Pete up into the branches. 'He's coming now.'

Then the man stretched up and put the bird on a branch, as high as he could reach. The mother bird called again. The baby bird fluttered his wings, then up, up, he went, trying very hard, till he reached home at last.

The man and Pete looked at each other. 'Will his Mummy be cross, do you think?' said Pete.

'I shouldn't think so,' said the man. 'She'll probably give him an extra big dinner.'

Pete thought for a moment. Then he said: 'That's what *my* Mummy would do. Give me jellies and custard and cakes and meringues. . . .'

And he nodded to the man, and wandered down the hill again, singing his own spring song.

'Spring ter-ring, ter-ring,
Spring ter-ring, ter-ring,

Ter-ring,
Ter-ring,
Buttercups and daisies.'

Yes, that was a special day.

ROOFS

WHEN I look out from my window high,
Hundreds of rooftops stretch to the sky
At every front door someone's ringing,
In every garden a bird is singing,
In every kitchen eggs are cooking,
From every window a child is looking

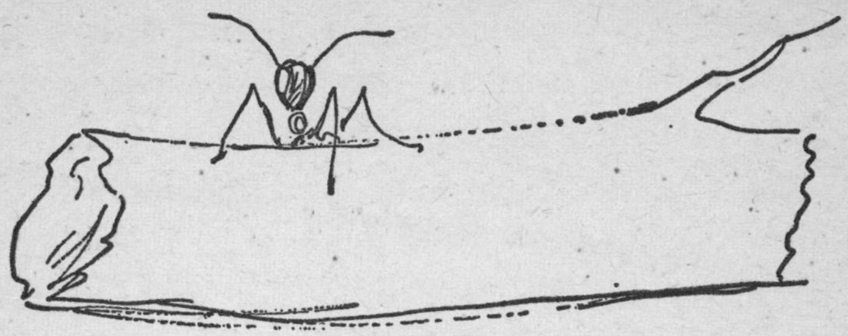

11

PETE AND THE WONDERFUL TAP

ONE day, Pete was looking for an ant. He knew where to look because he often saw ants. But today they seemed to be staying indoors. Pete looked and looked . . . and at last one came hurrying along.

'Where did you come from?' said Pete. 'Are you going in, or coming out?'

And he put a tiny stick in front of it, to see if it would go over it or under it.

The ant went over it, as if it were a very

high mountain. 'I would go under it,' said Pete, 'if I were an ant.'

While Pete was looking at the ant, he saw a dog watching him. He was a white dog, very fluffed-out, like raggedy cotton-wool.

He kept staring at Pete. And Pete looked at him from under his eyebrows, then looked at the ant again. When Pete looked again, from the corners of his eyes, secretly, the dog opened his mouth wide and laughed.

Pete slowly put out a hand, and kept it wide open, so that the dog could see there was

nothing in his hand that could hurt. He knew this was the right thing to do, because someone had told him. And the dog got up, and came over and licked it.

Then Pete said: 'Would you like to sit next to me? You can if you like.' And he patted the space next to him. The dog came and sat there.

The dog stuck out his tongue and panted, huh, huh, huh. Pete looked at him, and looked away. He wondered how it felt to do that. After a minute or two, he stuck out his tongue, too. Then both of them sat on the door-step, panting. Huh, huh, huh, huh.

But Pete got tired of this.

'Come on, dog,' he said. 'You're my dog, and you must come with me, and do whatever I tell you.' The dog got up.

As they walked along, Pete shouted: 'Bad dog, good dog, come *here*. Do that at *once*. Fetch it, fetch it.'

The dog didn't know what Pete was talking about, but he was a kind dog and didn't mind, so he kept on walking with Pete, and just didn't take any notice.

Then they began to run, and sometimes Pete ran in front of the dog, shouting: 'Come on, come *on*.' And sometimes Pete ran behind the dog, shouting: 'Come on, come *on*.' It was very nice both ways.

At last they came to a little low wall with a house behind it, and they rested. While they were resting, something said, 'Pete'. After a moment, it said it again. 'Pete.' Then it waited and said – 'Pete'.

'Who keeps saying that?' said Pete sternly.

And something said, 'Pete'. Pete wrinkled his brows and looked very fierce.

But the raggedy dog was sitting with his head on one side, looking at a tap that was fastened to the wall.

In a minute the tap said, 'Pete'. And there was a round wet spot below the tap, on the ground.

Pete stood beside the dog and watched too. First the tap got wet with the drop that was coming. Then the wetness grew into a little drop. Then it grew and grew until it was a ball. Then it began to shake . . . and shake . . . and shake . . . and at last it fell.

And when it felt itself falling, it tried to hold

on to the tap, but it couldn't. So it called out, 'Pete!' And the splash on the ground grew wetter and blacker.

Pete was pleased. He played a very good game with the tap, and the dog played too. The way they played it was this:

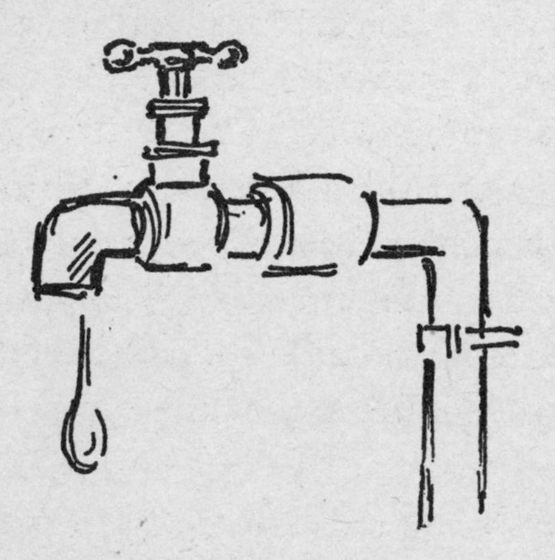

Pete put his hands over his face and started counting very fast. Then when the tap said 'Pete', the raggedy dog said, 'Out' (that was the way he barked). And that meant Pete should stop counting.

If he had got to fifty before he stopped, then Pete won.

And if he didn't get to fifty, then who won? Nobody.

Four times Pete played this game and won. The fifth time he counted up to fifty . . . up to sixty . . . up to seventy! And nothing happened.

Pete bent down and looked at the tap. He touched it with his finger. It was quite dry.

'Bother,' said Pete.

'Horrid thing,' said Pete.

'Just when I was winning,' said Pete.

He got hold of the handle and turned it round and round. But nothing happened. He made it simply *whizz* round and round – and then something did happen.

Someone said, 'HEY!'

Pete turned round. There was a man behind him. He had a big spanner. He pushed Pete to one side and started unscrewing the tap.

'You shouldn't push,' said Pete. 'You should say "Excuse me", you know that, don't you? Anyway, what are you doing to my tap? It kept saying "Pete" and I counted up to fifty, and I won every time, and I bet I'd have won again only it's stopped saying

"Pete", and now it's gone dry. And why are you taking it to pieces? Will you make it say "Pete" again?'

Then he sat down on the wall again and put his thumb in his mouth, because he had never had a tap that said 'Pete' before, and he was sad to lose it.

The man said nothing. He had stuck out the very tip of his tongue between his teeth, to help him unscrew the tap properly. And when Pete looked at the dog, he saw the dog had stuck out the tip of his tongue too.

So after a minute, Pete did the same. There they all sat, the three of them, with the tips of their tongues out.

Then Pete remembered he was cross with the man. So he said: 'Why are you spoiling my game, and messing up my tap, and sitting next to my dog?'

'Well,' said the man, still not looking at Pete, but only looking very hard at the tap, 'it may be your game, but it's *my* tap. *And* it's my dog.'

Pete was very surprised. He didn't say a word.

'His name is Trip,' the man went on. 'I call him that, because either he trips over me, or I trip over him.'

Pete thought about this. 'You should both look where you're going,' he said. 'I always do. What are you doing to the tap?'

The man said nothing for a bit. He was still trying to unscrew it. At last he said: 'I'm putting a new washer on it because it drips and drips.'

'But I like it to drip,' said Pete sadly. 'It says "Pete". That's my name.'

'Really?' said the man. 'What a clever tap!'

'So will you leave it?' asked Pete, hopefully.

'Well,' said the man, 'it's like this. This water comes miles and miles to get to this tap. It comes from rivers, and ponds, and streams, and at last it gets into this tap. You wouldn't want it all to pop out again, just to say "Pete", would you now?'

'Yes,' said Pete. 'I like it.'

'I know what you mean,' said the man, looking at him. 'I would like it if it said "Bert" (that's my name). And *he*' (he nodded to the dog), 'he would like it if it said "Trip".'

'Trip,' said Pete. 'I think it *did* say "Trip" as well.'

'But it didn't say "Bert" I suppose?' said the man sadly.

Pete thought. 'Mm,' he said, 'it did, just once.'

'That's grand,' said the man, looking very happy again, and finishing the tap. 'It's lucky you were here to listen to it, or we'd never have known. Now we can tell everyone about it when we go home for our dinners.'

'But it won't ever do it again, will it?' said Pete slowly. 'You've made it stop.'

Then the man came very close to Pete, and said, 'Suppose, just suppose, you were terribly thirsty and you wanted a drink. And you turned on the tap thinking "at last, I can have a drink". And no water came out, because it had dripped away, saying "Pete" all the time. Or "Trip" even. Or "Bert". What would you do then?'

'I'd have milk,' said Pete.

Then the man laughed. And the raggedy

dog opened his mouth and laughed too. So Pete did the same because they were his friends.

Then the man and the dog went up the path together, back to the house where they belonged. And Pete waved to them.

Just as they went inside, the sun came from behind the clouds. And there was Pete's shadow behind him.

'Well!' said Pete. 'I bet you'll never guess what I've seen. It's a secret, such a secret. And I'll never tell you!'

But his shadow didn't mind. It was still friends with Pete, and skipped beside him all the way home.

That was a special day.

12

PETE AND THE CIRCUS ELEPHANT

ONE morning, Pete went out straight after breakfast. It was very cold. The hedge was covered with thick white fur. 'Can you see?' said Pete to his shadow. 'That's snow.' But it wasn't. It was frost.

Pete pulled a leaf out of the hedge. It looked like a furry rabbit's ear. 'Will it tickle?' Pete wondered. So he put it against his cheek to see.

But it didn't tickle. It scratched. Pete put it back in the hedge where it lived.

The low wall next to the hedge was white and furry too. In the white there were little marks – arrow-marks. Pete knew they were arrows. 'They are pointing at something,' he told his shadow. 'Arrows always point. These arrows are pointing at the hedge.' And he nodded in an important way.

As he stood there, staring at the arrow-marks, he saw a robin looking at him. The robin was standing on the wall.

When the robin saw Pete was looking at him, he flew away. And there where the robin had been standing were two more arrow-marks. Pete looked at them. 'It's his feet,' he said. 'He has arrows on his feet, making all these arrow-marks.' Then he noticed that the robin's arrows pointed backwards. 'His feet are back to front,' he said. 'The silly!'

Now he thought no more about the robin. He went out of the gate, but his shadow would not hurry. It stayed inside the garden. 'I will shut you in,' said Pete. 'And then what d'you think?' But his shadow was always cleverer than Pete thought. It climbed right over the gate and came over on Pete's side. 'You see?' said Pete sternly. 'That will teach you.'

Pete was wearing a red and white striped hat, with a special bit to cover his ears, and a bobble on top. Pete's shadow had a hat too,

but his was plain. All Pete's shadow's clothes were plain, and all Pete's clothes were stripey and squiggley and full of colours.

Pete's breath came in little white clouds. He was very pleased with it. 'I'm a steam-engine!' he shouted. 'Huh. Huh. Hu-u-u-uh!'

And he started chugging down the road. And his shadow chugged along beside him, but he had no steam. Only Pete had steam.

Now when Pete was standing still on the pavement, waiting for passengers and getting his breath back, he heard a strange noise. While he was listening he went on saying 'Chshshshshshsh!' to himself, because he hadn't stopped playing trains yet.

It was an exciting noise. 'D-d-rum! D-d-rum!' Now Pete knew what it was. It was a band.

He dashed to the edge of the pavement, so that he could see right down the road. It wasn't only a band. There were four elephants coming, and two clowns, and a girl on a pale yellow horse. It was a circus procession.

Pete stared.

One of the elephants was walking close to

the pavement where Pete was standing. Pete watched him coming, nearer and nearer. 'How big he is,' thought Pete. 'Soon I will see his tail. It will be an enormous tail, like a tree, but feathery.'

But the elephant only had a tiny tail.

Pete was very sad when he saw it.

So he looked at the elephant's feet instead. They went up and down, blump, blump, instead of straight forward like Pete's feet. Pete began to walk like an elephant. Blump, blump.

Suddenly, while he was looking sideways at

the real elephant's feet, the elephant took off Pete's hat.

He took it by the bobble with his long curly trunk, and he started to put it in his mouth. 'No,' shouted the man on his back. 'Give it to me, you bad one!'

So the elephant gave the hat to the man on his back, and the man took it and gave it to a clown who was walking alongside, and the clown put it back again on Pete's head.

Pete stood quite still. All the children who had been walking and skipping along with the band passed him by, the band faded away, even the drums were only whispering, whispering, until there was nothing to hear any more. Still Pete stood there. And his shadow lay down on the ground and waited.

Then Pete slowly put his hand to his head. His hat was there. Pete felt all over it, slowly. The bobble was wet, where the elephant had held it.

'It's *my* hat,' said Pete, in a whisper.

Then he said it again, more fiercely and a little bit louder. 'It's *my* hat!'

Then he shouted down the road very angrily

to the elephant, who was a long, long way off. 'IT'S *MY* HAT!' And he shouted again, 'IT'S *MY* HAT, YOU BIG BAD ELEPHANT! DO YOU HEAR ME! MY *GOODNESS*!'

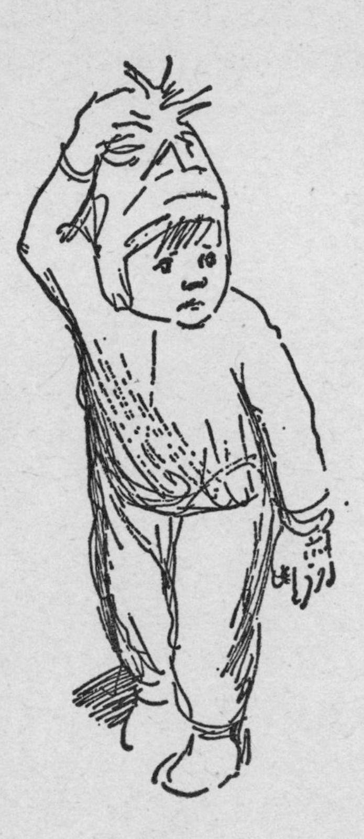

And with a very stern face, and his forehead all wrinkled, Pete opened his garden gate again. 'My *goodness*!' he said sternly to his shadow. 'That will teach you!'

And his shadow was so frightened at Pete's grand voice that he slipped inside the gate at once. And Pete shut it behind them.

That was a very special day indeed.

LULLABY

WHAT'S the matter, Teddy,
What can make you cry?
Are you frightened of the thunder
Coming from the sky?

Don't you cry, my Teddy,
Snuggle down here deep.
I will softly sing to you
Until you're fast asleep.